# Trucks Trucks Trucks Trucks Trucks Trucks

## BY PETER SÍS

Greenwillow Books · New York

**For Cristina Melfi**
**and Kathy Williams,**
**teachers at Creative Steps**

Printed in Singapore by Tien Wah Press
First Edition   10 9 8 7 6 5 4 3 2 1

Library of Congress
Cataloging-in-Publication Data
Sís, Peter
Trucks, trucks, trucks / by Peter Sís.
    p.    cm.
Summary: A little boy cleans up his room
using a variety of trucks and gives a one-
word description of their work such as
hauling, plowing, and loading. Features
a gate-fold illustration that opens into
a three-page spread.
ISBN 0-688-16276-2    1. Toy and
movable books—Specimens.
[1. Trucks—Fiction.
2. Toy and movable books.]
I. Title   PZ7.S6219Tr
1999   [E]—dc21
98-4482
CIP   AC

**Matt, will you pick up your trucks?**

DIGGING

PLOWING

PUSHING

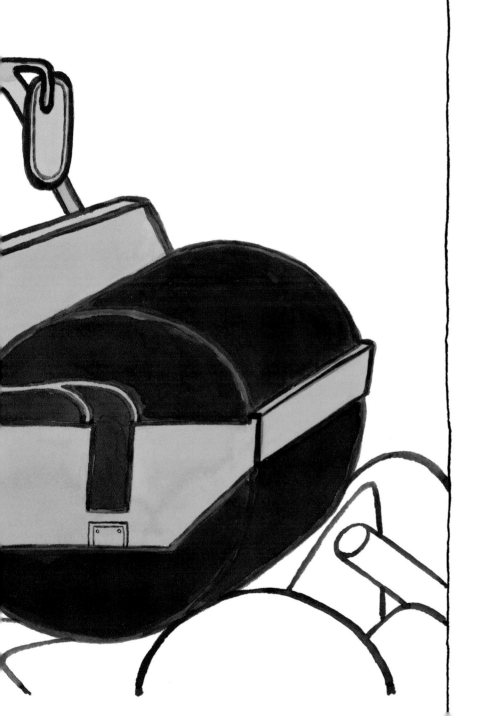

ROLLING

**SCOOOPING**

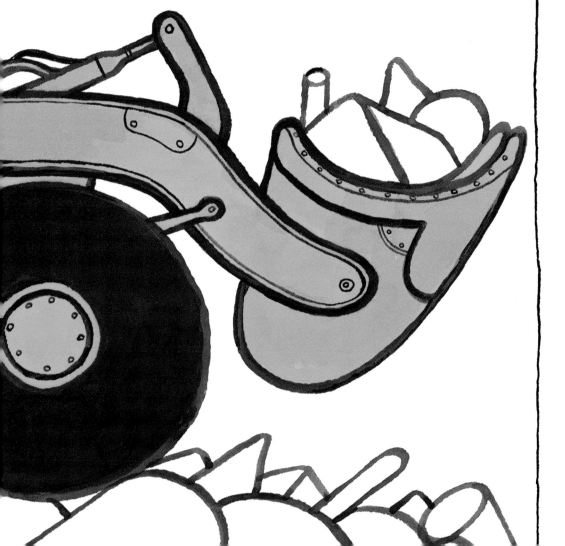

LOADING

**HAULING**

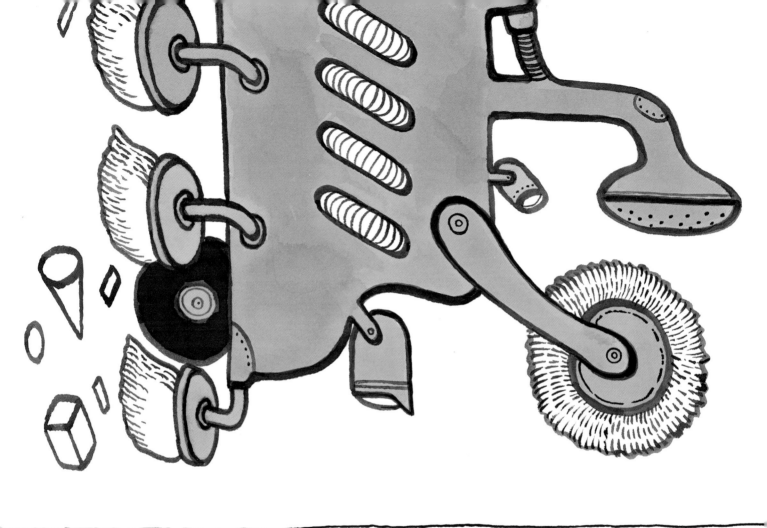

# SWEEPING

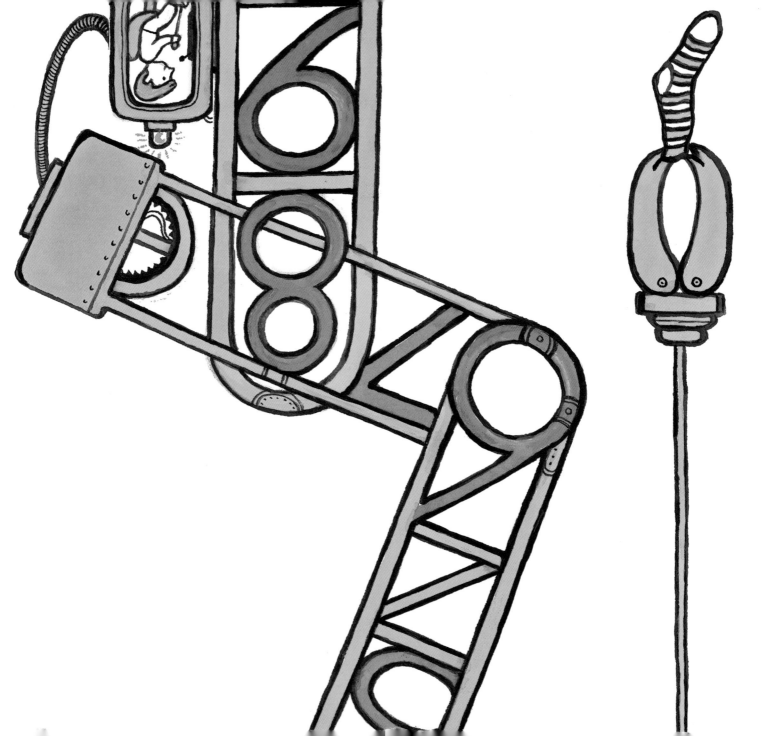

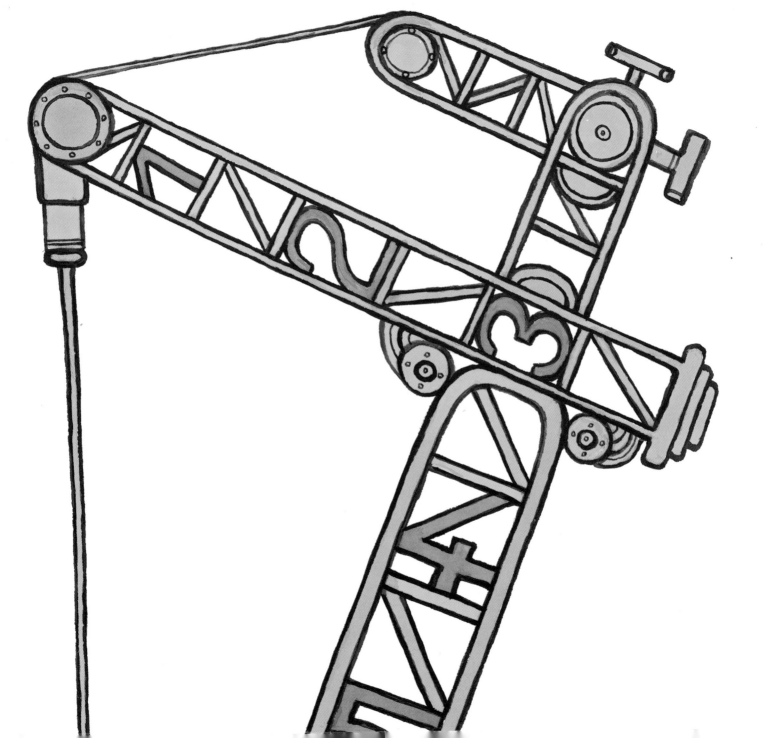

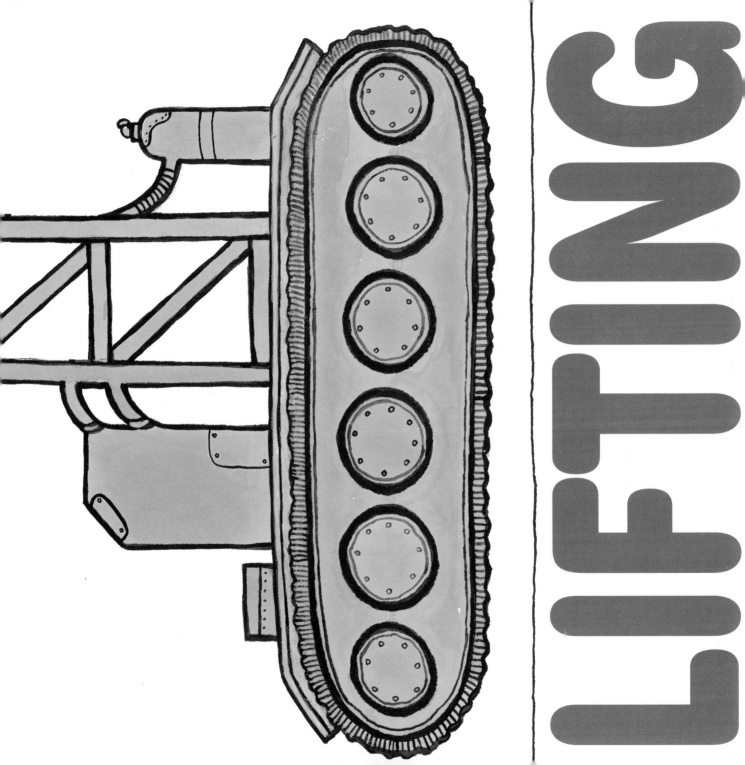

LIFTING

Good job, Matt. Now let's go out.